Peter Spit a Seed at Sue

by Jackie French Koller   illustrated by John Manders

VIKING

VIKING

Published by Penguin Group

Penguin Young Readers Group, 345 Hudson Street, New York, New York 10014, U.S.A.

Penguin Group (Canada), 90 Eglinton Avenue East, Suite 700, Toronto, Ontario, Canada M4P 2Y3

(a division of Pearson Penguin Canada Inc.)

Penguin Books Ltd, 80 Strand, London WC2R 0RL, England

Penguin Ireland, 25 St Stephen's Green, Dublin 2, Ireland (a division of Penguin Books Ltd)

Penguin Group (Australia), 250 Camberwell Road, Camberwell, Victoria 3124, Australia

(a division of Pearson Australia Group Pty Ltd)

Penguin Books India Pvt Ltd, 11 Community Centre, Panchsheel Park, New Delhi – 110 017, India

Penguin Group (NZ), 67 Apollo Drive, Rosedale, North Shore 0632, New Zealand

(a division of Pearson New Zealand Ltd)

Penguin Books (South Africa) (Pty) Ltd, 24 Sturdee Avenue, Rosebank,

Johannesburg 2196, South Africa

Penguin Books Ltd, Registered Offices: 80 Strand, London WC2R 0RL, England

First published in 2008 by Viking, a division of Penguin Young Readers Group

10   9   8   7   6   5   4   3   2   1

Text copyright © Jackie French Koller, 2008
Illustrations copyright © John Manders, 2008

LIBRARY OF CONGRESS CATALOGING-IN-PUBLICATION DATA IS AVAILABLE
ISBN: 978-0-670-06309-3

Manufactured in China   Set in Rockwell Regular   Book design by Jim Hoover

For dear little Anna,
who taught me how much fun spitting could be!
—J.F.K.

To Stanley Laurel and Oliver Hardy
these pictures are humbly dedicated.
—J.M.

Mary Lou and I were bored
And so were Pete and Sue next door.
Over they came and we were four.

Four bored kids on a boring porch,
Watching a bug crawl across the floor.

Just then we heard a fella yellin'—he was sellin' watermelon!

Melons! Icy cold and sweet.
Melons! What a perfect treat!
Just the thing four kids could use
To chase away their boring blues.

We **chomped** and **Slurped**
And **gulped** and **burped.**
Then Peter spit a seed at Sue,
Which hit her cheek and stuck like glue.

Susie **spit** one back at Pete,
Which struck and stuck right on his seat.

Pete spit two at Mary Lou.
How could I help but join in, too?

"C'mon!" I yelled to Mary Lou,
"You pepper Pete! I'll splatter Sue!"

Then seeds were flyin' everywhere,
Zippin', zingin' through the air.
Seeds were plastered to our clothes.
Seeds were stuck between our toes.

Seeds were tangled in our hair.
Seeds got **down** our **underwear!**

Off we ran across the yard,
Spitting fast and spitting hard.
The laundry fluttered in the breeze
As seeds buzzed through the air like bees.

Soon our sheets had **polka dots**
And Dad's shorts sported leopard spots.

We still could hear that fella yellin,'
"Come and get your watermelon!"
He was in the village square.
Seconds later we were there,
Gobbling up a new supply.
We slurped 'em in and let 'em fly!

Off we swooped across the square
Raining seeds down everywhere.
Oops! One hit the traffic cop.

We thought for sure he'd make us stop,
But then he got an impish grin,
Grabbed a slice, and **plunged right in!**

A camp bus rumbled up and stopped,
And out of doors and windows popped
Sixty children shouting, "Yum!
Watermelon! Give us some!"

Before we knew it, **everyone**
Was clamoring to join the fun.

Mailmen, nannies, grocery clerks,
Barbers, butchers, soda jerks,
Teachers, preachers, hard-hat guys,
Even dudes in suits and ties.

Through the thick and thin of it
We spit and spit and spit and spit,
Till from a limo stepped the mayor,
Who fixed us with a steely stare.

"Enough!" she boomed.
"Just look around!
What have you DONE
To our poor town?"

It was a sight, I must confess,
A spitty, spotty, dotty mess.

We bowed our heads and took the blame.
We swore we'd never spit again,
And vowed to clean it up
But then ...

A baker and his cart went by
And with a **twinkle** in her eye,

The mayor grabbed a whipped-cream pie. **"Gotcha!"** she cried, and let it fly!

I wiped the cream out of my eyes
And looked at her in great surprise.
She laughed and picked up two more pies.

"Pie fight!" cried Pete. "Yahoo! Me, too!"
He grabbed a pie and so did Sue.

Then pies were flyin' everywhere.
Zippin', zingin' through the air.
I turned and grinned at Mary Lou.
How could we help but join in, too?